WILD animal ABC

Story and illustrations by P.J. Rankin Hults

Schiffer Kids™

4880 Lower Valley Road, Atglen, PA 19310

Allen the Aardvark
Is an adventurous soul.
He explores the world
From the North to South Pole.

Bb

Bert the Bear
Is strong and brave.
He's always looking
For someone to save.

Chester the Chipmunk
Is a curious guy.
He loves to explore
And always asks, "Why?"

Dd

Delilah the Dolphin
Dives deep in the sea.
When she is swimming
She's very carefree.

Ee

Ella the Elephant
Is eager to turn eight.
She's having a party
To celebrate.

THE

FOXY FASHION

JOURNAL

ISSUE 5

FANTASTIC FASHIONS for the fab, finicky fox

FUN FALL FEATURES

FUNKY • FETCHING • FANCY

Frederick the Fox
Is a fashionable chap.
He looks really fab
In his gray tweed cap.

Genevieve the Giraffe
Likes to spread glee.
She's invited friends
For cookies and tea.

Hh

Hester the Hedgehog
Is so very happy.
Her new summer hat
Makes her feel snappy.

Ingrid the Ibis
Imagines what she'll create.
With her paint and brushes,
Her art will be great.

Jordy the Jewelfish
Gives her tail a joyful swish.
When she blows a bubble,
She sends a special wish.

Kyle the Kangaroo
Shows kindness to all.
It's simple to say, "Hello"
Whether you're big or small.

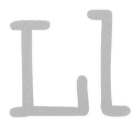

Lonnie the Leopard
Is well liked by his friends.
They go on a safari
He hopes never ends.

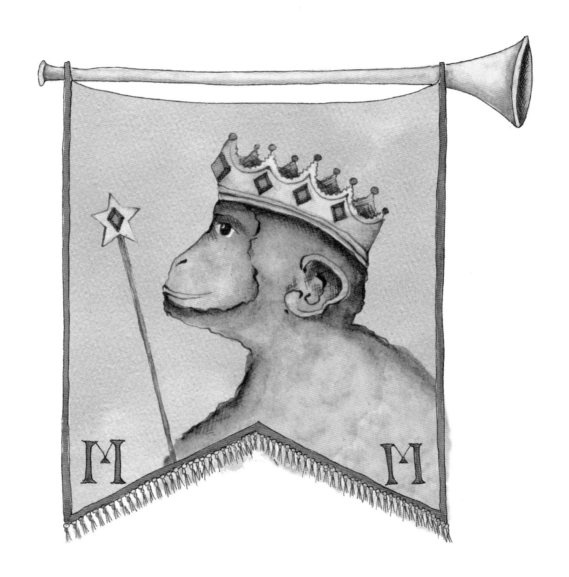

Mm

Maurice the Monkey
Is majestic and royal.
All of his subjects
Are very loyal.

Nn

Nate the Newt
And his neighbor James
Pretend they are wizards
And play magic games.

NEW PAPER HATS ARE FUN
MAKE SOME AND WEAR FOR
PICTURES. GREAT MEMORIES.

Ollie the Octopus
Is overjoyed with his hat.
Made of folded paper
So it won't fall flat.

P p

Professor Phineas Penguin
Has a passion for education.
He reads lots of books,
Even on his vacation.

Quincy the Quail
Writes a quirky rhyme.
She carries a quill
To jot thoughts any time.

Rr

Ralph the Rhinoceros
Respects everyone.
Saying please and thank you
Is polite and fun.

Seymour the Seahorse
And his silly pirate friends
Like to sing and dance
Until the daylight ends.

Tt

Theodore the Tiger
May look rather tame,
But he's a toe-tickler
Of tremendous fame.

Uu

Uma the Unicorn
Is a unique creature.
Her rainbow colors
Are her most enchanting feature.

DICTIONARY

Vinny the Vulture
Likes his dictionary.
He won his class spelling bee
With his vast vocabulary.

Wilhelmina the Whale
Is talented and witty.
She can balance her umbrella
And sing a little ditty.

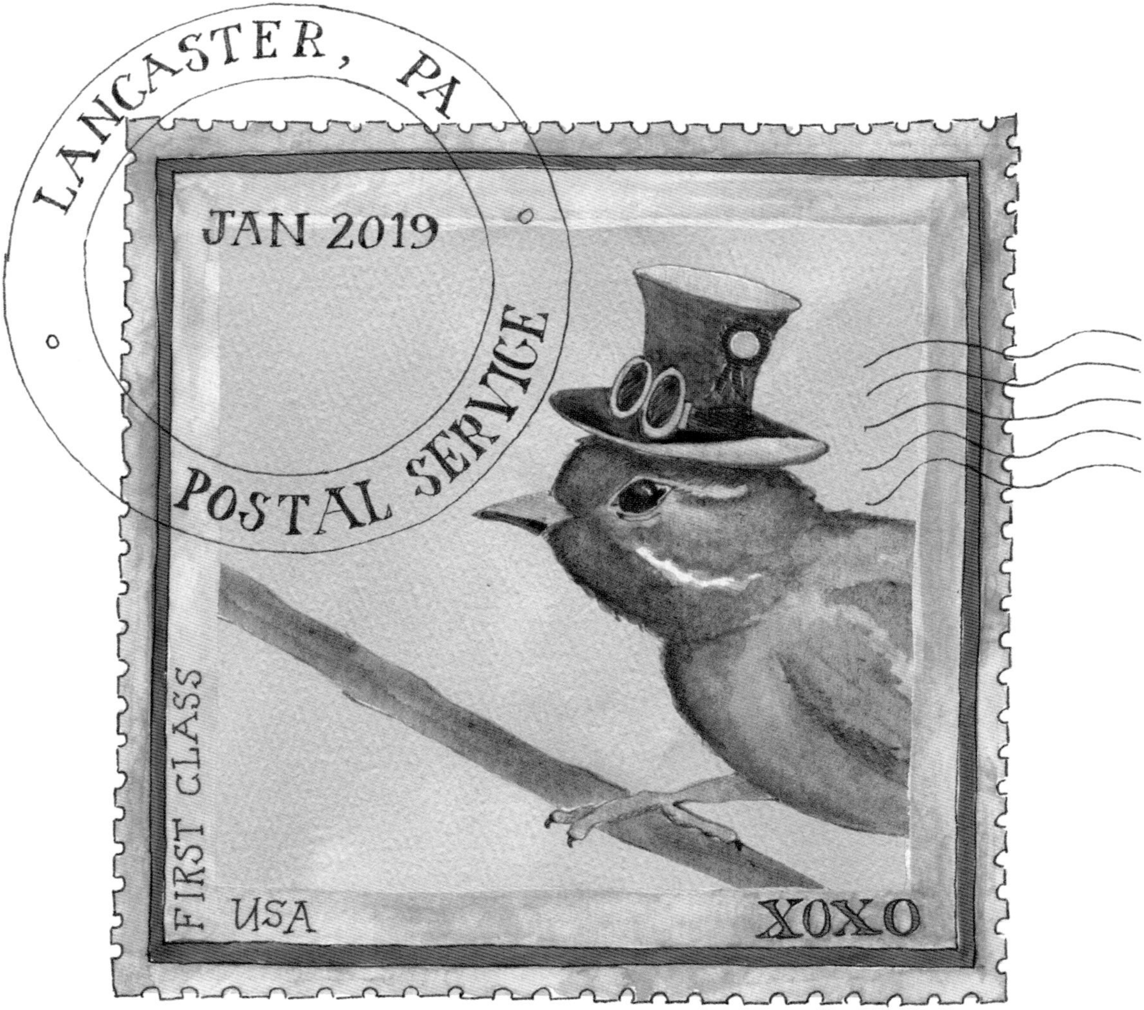
LANCASTER, PA
POSTAL SERVICE
JAN 2019
FIRST CLASS
USA
XOXO

Xylo the Xenops
Sends letters with kisses XXX
To all the friends and family
He loves and misses.

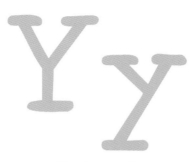

Yarnell the Yak
Yawns in the sun.
He takes a nap
After his work is done.

Zz

Zach the Zebra
Puts on his hat.
He does a zany little dance
Tappity-tap-tap.

Glossary
of Hats and
Animal Facts

Allen the Aardvark has a long snout to sniff out his dinner of ants and termites.
He has a sticky tongue to pick them up.
He can use his claws to dig a hole in the ground and cover himself with dirt when he wants to hide.
Where do you like to hide?

Bert the Bear has lots of cousins in all colors.
The grizzly bear is brown, the panda bear is black and white, the polar bear is white, and there is also a black bear.
Bert can climb trees and he swims really well.
He can run 30 miles per hour. That's very fast.
How fast can you run?

Chester the Chipmunk likes to eat seeds, nuts, fruit, and acorns.
He gathers food in his cheek pouches.
He can collect 150 acorns a day.
Do you ever collect acorns?

Delilah the Dolphin is a mammal that lives in the sea.
She has great hearing and communicates with other dolphins using clicks and whistles.
Can you whistle?

Ella the Elephant is the largest land mammal.
She has a long trunk for breathing and she uses it to put food and water in her mouth.
Ella and her family live in groups called herds and are very social.
Do you think they have birthday parties?

Frederick the Fox is part of the dog family but he can be very cunning and sometimes a nuisance.
He is a common red fox.
His fur is red, but foxes come in lots of colors, including white, brown, black, gray, blonde, and sandy.
What color is your hair?

Genevieve the Giraffe is the tallest mammal.
She has a long tongue to reach her food and eats 75 pounds of food a day.
She sleeps very little, sometimes only 30 minutes a day.
I hope you eat less and sleep more than Genevieve.

Hester the Hedgehog is a spiny mammal and can have up to 5,000 spines.
She lives under bushes and in dens in the ground.
She has poor eyesight, so she depends on hearing and smell to navigate.
Can you find your way around your house with your eyes closed, using only touch, smell, and sound?

Ingrid the Ibis is a scarlet Ibis, because the shellfish she eats have a substance called carotenoids, which make her feathers red.
She lives in a large flock for safety.
Her flock has other birds like storks, herons, spoonbills, egrets, and ducks. They are all friends.
Does your flock have different kinds of friends?

Jordy the Jewelfish lives in Africa and can be found in rivers and streams where plants hang over the water.
Jewelfish usually live in pairs.
She is a beautiful creature.
I am sure you are beautiful too!

Kyle the Kangaroo is a marsupial.
That's an animal that can carry their baby in a pouch on their belly.
He lives in Australia.
He hops on his powerful back legs.
Can you hop?

Lonnie the Leopard has short legs and a long body.
He can run 36 miles per hour.
That's even faster than Bert.
His fur has spots that help him hide in the jungle.
He likes to climb trees and rest in the branches.
Do you like to climb trees?

Maurice the Monkey lives in the trees.
He is a primate and has a tail that allows him to
grasp and hold objects.
His tail helps him to hold the branches of a tree when he is
reaching for fruit, nuts, leaves and seeds.
His favorite food is bananas.
Do you like bananas?

Nate the Newt is an amphibian.
He has a body like a lizard.
His home is in the Northern Hemisphere.
He lives in the water or the damp areas of land by the water.
He sleeps all winter under the logs or stones or sometimes at the
bottom of the pond.
That is a very long time to sleep.

Ollie the Octopus has eight arms with suckers called tentacles to help him pick things up.
He has a very good sense of touch.
He lives in the ocean and eats fish, crabs, and mollusks.
Do you like the ocean?

Professor Phineas Penguin is an aquatic bird that cannot fly.
He walks upright on two legs and waddles as he walks.
He spends half of his time on land and half in the water.
He is an impressive swimmer.
Do you like to swim?

Quincy the Quail is a small, short-tailed bird. She wears a topknot of feathers.
She can fly 30 miles per hour.
She takes dust baths by burrowing in the soft dirt, then wiggling and flapping her wings.
A bath in the dirt? That's silly.

Ralph the Rhinoceros weighs more than 2,200 pounds. That's big!
His name "Rhino" means nose horn.
His horn is made of keratin, the same material as your fingernails.
He is a vegetarian, so he must eat a lot of plants and vegetables.
Do you like to eat your vegetables?

Seymour the Seahorse is a very slow swimmer.
He lives in the ocean in the coral reefs, seagrass beds,
and mangrove roots.
He can change color to blend in with his surroundings.
How fun would it be to change colors?
What's your favorite color?

Theodore the Tiger is the biggest species in
the cat family.
He can grow up to 11 feet long and weigh 600 pounds.
He has a unique set of stripes in orange,
black, and white.
What colors would your stripes be?

Uma the Unicorn is a good and mystical creature that
lives in our imagination.
She looks like a horse with a horn.
She and her friends come in every color and
many patterns.
Have you ever seen a unicorn?

Vinny the Vulture is called nature's garbage man
because he can eat food that other animals cannot eat.
He helps keep the earth clean.
He has strong wings and can glide in the sky for hours.
Can you imagine gliding in the sky for hours?

Wilhelmina the Whale is a marine mammal.
She is intelligent and lives in a family.
She and her family communicate by tail slapping, high-pitched squeaks, clicks, and whistles.
They can tell others if they find food or see danger.
She can weigh up to 150 tons.
That is how much an airplane weighs.
How much do you weigh?

Xylo the Xenops is a cool little bird that lives in the rainforest.
He is only 5 inches long.
He lives in tree holes and eats insects.
Do you ever wonder who lives in tree holes?

Yarnell the Yak has horns and long, thick fur to keep him warm.
He lives in mountainous Tibet.
He is a friendly mammal that lives on a farm and works with humans.
Do you know any farmers?

Zach the Zebra is a wild horse with unique black and white stripes.
He lives with his family in Africa.
He can run 40 miles per hour.
He zigzags as he runs so no one can catch him.
Can you zigzag when you run?

Who am I?

Starting each sentence with "I wear...,"
can you guess why each hat or accessory is important?

A- a desert hat to keep the sun off my head while searching for ants.

B- a park ranger hat because I live in the woods and like to help others.

C- an acorn for a hat in case I need a snack.

D- goggles and a snorkel because I swim in the ocean.

E- my party hat because it is my birthday.

F- a newsboy cap because it is stylish and I am in the news.

G- my fancy pillbox hat for afternoon tea.

H- my straw hat to spend days in the garden.

I- a Victorian ladies hat because I am an artist and creative character.

J- a bubble blower to send out good wishes.

K- a bush hat because I come from Australia.

L- a safari hat so I am always ready for adventure.

M- a crown that is fit for a king.

N- a wizard's hat to play magic games.

O- a folded-paper sailor's hat.

P- a graduation cap because I pass every grade.

Q- a bonnet to keep my quill handy.

R- a bowler hat because I am a respectful gent.

S- a pirate hat when I sing and dance with my friends.

T- a bucket hat because it reminds me of my gentle grandpa with a silly side.

U- a flower wreath on my head just because it is pretty.

V- a jester hat because I am smart and funny too.

W- an umbrella because when I breathe, I spout water in the air.

X- this hat while writing letters to my steampunk friends.

Y- a Tibetan fur hat because it is cold where I live.

Z- a top hat when I get dressed up for my recital.

To my friends and family for their
encouragement and assistance.
To June and Naomi, our newest readers.
To John, for everything.

Pam Hults has always enjoyed art and looking for the creative view, from childhood and through school, ending with a BA in art education from Kutztown University. Pam spent 40 years as a traditional Pennsylvania folk artist in watercolor and paper cutting but always wanted to publish a children's book, and now it has become a reality because she never gave up on her dream. The most important values in Pam's life are faith, family (which includes her pets), and her art. Pam and her family are from Lancaster County, Pennsylvania.

ISBN: 978-0-7643-6119-7
Printed in China

Published by Schiffer Kids
An imprint of Schiffer Publishing, Ltd.
4880 Lower Valley Road
Atglen, PA 19310
Phone: (610) 593-1777; Fax: (610) 593-2002
E-mail: Info@schifferbooks.com
Web: www.schifferbooks.com

For our complete selection of fine books on this and related subjects, please visit our website at www.schifferbooks.com. You may also write for a free catalog.

Schiffer Publishing's titles are available at special discounts for bulk purchases for sales promotions or premiums. Special editions, including personalized covers, corporate imprints, and excerpts, can be created in large quantities for special needs. For more information, contact the publisher.